DREAMWORKS

KUNG FU PANDA
2

KABOOM OF DOOM

PRICE STERN SLOAN
Published by the Penguin Group
Penguin Group (USA) Inc., 375 Hudson Street, New York, New York 10014, USA
Penguin Group (Canada), 90 Eglinton Avenue East, Suite 700, Toronto, Ontario M4P 2Y3, Canada
(a division of Pearson Penguin Canada Inc.)
Penguin Books Ltd., 80 Strand, London WC2R 0RL, England
Penguin Group Ireland, 25 St. Stephen's Green, Dublin 2, Ireland (a division of Penguin Books Ltd.)
Penguin Group (Australia), 250 Camberwell Road, Camberwell, Victoria 3124, Australia
(a division of Pearson Australia Group Pty. Ltd.)
Penguin Books India Pvt. Ltd., 11 Community Centre, Panchsheel Park, New Delhi—110 017, India
Penguin Group (NZ), 67 Apollo Drive, Rosedale, Auckland 0632, New Zealand
(a division of Pearson New Zealand Ltd.)
Penguin Books (South Africa) (Pty.) Ltd., 24 Sturdee Avenue, Rosebank,
Johannesburg 2196, South Africa

Penguin Books Ltd., Registered Offices: 80 Strand, London WC2R 0RL, England

Kung Fu Panda 2 ™ & © 2011 DreamWorks Animation L.L.C. Kung Fu Panda ® DreamWorks
Animation L.L.C. Published by Price Stern Sloan, a division of Penguin Young Readers Group,
345 Hudson Street, New York, New York, 10014. PSS! is a registered trademark of
Penguin Group (USA) Inc. Printed in the U.S.A.

ISBN 978-0-8431-9861-4   10 9 8 7 6 5 4 3 2 1

KABOOM OF DOOM

by Cathy Hapka

PSS!
PRICE STERN SLOAN
An Imprint of Penguin Group (USA) Inc.

Po was the legendary Dragon Warrior. He
and the Furious Five protected the Valley of
Peace with their awesome kung fu skills.

One day, when a group of wolf bandits
attacked a village, Po and the Five went to
help.

As Po fought Boss Wolf, he spotted an eye-shaped symbol on the wolf's uniform. Suddenly, a strange vision flashed in his mind.

He saw tiny panda hands reaching for a panda mother.

Po was distracted, and the wolf bandits escaped.

The Five gathered around their friend.

"What happened?" Tigress asked.

Po shook his head. "I don't know."

Po couldn't stop thinking about his childhood memory. He went to his father's noodle shop.

"Dad," Po said. "Where did I come from?"

Mr. Ping decided it was time to tell Po the truth. "You might have been . . . kind of . . . adopted," he said.

Mr. Ping pulled out a radish basket. "You came from this," he said. "Years ago, I went out to the back to where my vegetables had just been delivered. Only there were no radishes. Just a very hungry baby panda."

Po was shocked. He couldn't believe his
parents had left him.

"Your story may not have a happy
beginning," Mr. Ping said. "But look how it's
turned out. You've got me, you've got kung
fu, you've got noodles."

But Po wondered if that was enough.

Meanwhile, many miles away, a peacock named Lord Shen arrived in Gongmen City where his family had ruled long ago. "Leave my house," he ordered the current rulers, Masters Rhino, Ox, and Croc.

But the great kung fu masters refused to go. Shen used a huge, terrible cannon against Master Rhino. All that remained was his hammer.

Shen and his army moved into Peacock's Palace.

"All of China will bow before me!" Shen said.

But Soothsayer warned him that a great warrior of black and white would defeat him.

When Shifu heard what had happened, he sent Po and the Five to Gongmen City.

On the journey, Po told Tigress that his dad wasn't his real dad. Tigress tried to help Po focus and find Inner Peace as Master Shifu had instructed.

When they arrived in Gongmen City, Po and the Five saw wolf soldiers everywhere.

Po saw Boss Wolf climb into a rickshaw. Po and the Five chased him to Shen's Palace.

At the Palace, they were outnumbered by the wolf army.

"We surrender!" Po said.

The wolves took Po and the Five to see Shen.

As Po and the Five were led to the Palace,
Po thought about Master Rhino. What could
Shen have that would defeat kung fu?

Po had a plan. But first he had to face his old enemy . . . stairs. Finally, with the help of a massive gorilla, Po entered Shen's throne room.

Shen was waiting for his guests. A large cannon stood beside him.

Shen instructed his guards to light the cannon.

Mantis was out of his cage! He put out the cannon's fuse as Viper freed Po and the Five.

Finally Po faced Shen.

Then he saw Shen's feathers. A red eye! Po had another vision: Shen had been there the night Po's parents left him!

With Po distracted, Shen jumped out
the window and raced across town to
the Fireworks Factory. He aimed rows of
cannons at the Palace and fired. The Palace
collapsed in flames.

Po and the Five escaped just in time.

The Five were upset. Tigress demanded that Po tell them the truth.

"You had Shen," she said. "What happened?"

Po told his friends about the red eye and his memories.

Tigress understood, but she wanted Po to stay safe. She told him to stay behind while the Five battled Shen.

The Five set off for Shen's Fireworks Factory.
The place was crawling with guards, so they set
up a careful plan of attack.

Po had gone to the Fireworks Factory, too. And he had found Shen.

The peacock laughed. "Your parents didn't love you!" he told Po.

Then Shen lit a cannon. *Kaboom!*

Po was blasted out of the factory. He landed in a river, where Soothsayer rescued him.

The old goat was very kind. She wanted to help Po remember his past.

Long ago, Po had lived in the panda village with his parents. It was a peaceful, happy place until Soothsayer read Shen's fate. She had told the peacock that a panda would stand in his way on his path to glory.

When Po was just a baby, Shen and his army had invaded the panda village and set fire to the homes.

Now Po understood. His parents hadn't abandoned him. His mother had hid him in the radish basket to save him!

Knowing the truth helped Po find Inner Peace. He balanced a single water drop in his hand as Master Shifu had taught him. The drop didn't break.

Po raced back to Gongmen City. Together,
he and the Five were ready to take on Shen
and his army.

Master Shifu and the kung fu masters
came to help with the battle.

Po used Shifu's lesson on Inner Peace to catch the cannonballs fired by Shen. Then he launched them back at the peacock and his army. Soon Shen and his cannons were destroyed.

Po returned to his father's noodle shop. His father was waiting for him.

"I know who I am," Po told his dad. "I am your son."

Mr. Ping hugged his son. Then they went inside to cook noodles together.